The Princess Tales

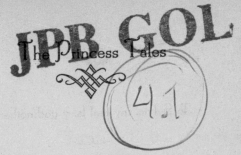

Princess Sonora and the Long Sleep

Gail Carson Levine

ILLUSTRATED BY Mark Elliott

SCHOLASTIC INC.

New York Toronto London Auckland Sydney
Mexico City New Delhi Hong Kong

To Sylvia, my real fairy godmother

—G.C.L.

ISBN 0-439-26502-9

Text copyright © 1999 by Gail Carson Levine.
Illustrations copyright © 1999 by Mark Elliott. All rights reserved.
Published by Scholastic Inc., 555 Broadway, New York, NY 10012,
by arrangement with HarperCollins Publishers.
SCHOLASTIC and associated logos are trademarks and/or
registered trademarks of Scholastic Inc.

12 11 10 9 8 7 6 5 4 3 2 1   1 2 3 4 5 6/0

Printed in the U.S.A.   01

First Scholastic printing, January 2001

Typography by Michele Tupper

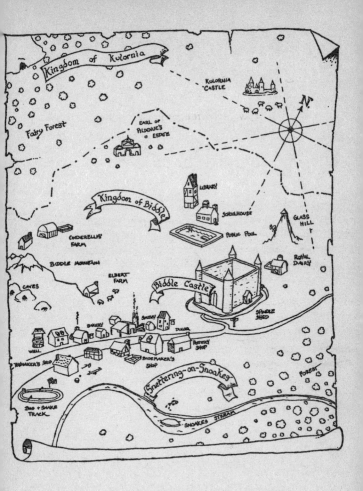

One

What a hideous baby, the fairy Arabella thought. She said, "My gift to Sonora is beauty." She touched the baby's yellow squooshed-up face with her wand.

The baby began to change. Her scrawny arms and legs became plump, and her blotchy yellow skin turned pink. Her pointy head became round. Honey-colored ringlets appeared on her scalp.

Ouch! It hurt to have your body change shape and to grow hair on your head in ten seconds. Sonora wailed.

1

King Humphrey II of Biddle thought, Why did the fairy do that? As his first-born child—as his lovey dovey oodle boodle baby—she had been fine the way she was. But he bowed low to the fairy. "Thank you, Arabella. What a wonderful gift." A person could get into a lot of trouble for failing to thank a fairy.

Queen Hermione II picked up the yowling baby and cuddled her. Then she curtsied deeply and thanked the fairy too, even though she wanted to wail along with her daughter. *Sonora looks six months old,* the queen thought. *I wanted to watch her grow.*

Gradually Sonora stopped crying, and her mother put her back into the gilded cradle. Time for the second fairy gift.

The fairy Allegra waved her wand over the baby. "I give Sonora the gift of a loving heart."

Something was happening again, Sonora realized. But this was better. This didn't hurt. She pictured the tall being and the soft being who fed her and held her and made noises to her. They were nice! She loved them! She said, "Goo," and blew a wet bubble.

Adorable! King Humphrey II thought.

Sweet! Queen Hermione II thought.

"My turn!" The fairy Adalissia stepped up to the cradle.

Adalissia gave Sonora gracefulness. Then the fairy Annadora gave her good health, and the fairy Antonetta made her the smartest human in the world.

Not much changed when Sonora got good health, since she was healthy already. And not much changed when she got gracefulness, because month-old babies don't have much opportunity to be graceful. But something did happen

3

when Antonetta made her a smart person. Sonora listened more closely when the nice beings thanked the fairy. She noticed her own name and knew that she'd heard it before.

Aurora, the sixth fairy, was flustered. She had planned to make Sonora the smartest person in the world, but that miserable Antonetta had stolen her gift. Now what could she give the baby? She could make the child beautiful. But no, Arabella had already used that one. Adalissia had done gracefulness. What was left? They were all looking at her. They were laughing behind their sympathetic faces, glad they had been at the head of the line.

"Er . . ." Aurora waved her wand vaguely. Then she had it. It was so simple. It was much better than Antonetta's.

4

She leaned over the cradle and touched Sonora on the nose with her wand. "My gift is brilliance. Sonora is ten times as smart as any human in the world." There.

Sonora felt something happen again, a tickle and a little shake inside her head. Then—it was done. She closed her eyes to think, really think, for the first time. She listened to the noise the tall being was making. She remembered all the noises people had made with their mouths since she'd been born. Some of the noises sounded alike. Some of them always went together.

Now the soft being was making noises. They were words! The noises were words. She was thanking the fairy for her gift. She was hoping that Sonora (that's me! that's me!) would use her extraordinary intelligence well.

Sonora opened her eyes. The soft being was her mother. She was beautiful, with her big brown eyes and those lips that liked to smile at Sonora. Of course she loved her mother, since the fairy had just given her a loving heart. Sonora wondered why the fairy had done that. Didn't she think Sonora might be naturally loving?

The fairy Adrianna came forward to the cradle. "My gift—"

The door to the royal nursery flew open. Adrianna gasped. The other fairies gasped. King Humphrey II gasped. Queen Hermione II gasped.

Sonora heard the gasps, but she could see only the things right above her, such as the pink dragon-shaped balloon that hung over the cradle. She thought, Why couldn't these fairies have given me something useful, like the ability to sit up and see what's going on?

A new fairy came in. She looked like all the others. Tall, with rubbery-looking wings, surrounded by a flickering rainbow of lights. Smiling like the others had been till a second ago.

Queen Hermione II rushed to the newcomer. "Belladonna! We're honored." In her mind she shouted, Don't hurt my baby! Don't hurt Sonora!

The fairy looked around the room. "Pretty nursery," she cooed in an extra-sweet voice. "Cuddly stuffed unicorn. Handsome dollcastle." She looked in the cradle. "Beautiful baby."

She looks angry, Sonora thought. You didn't have to be a genius to see that.

Belladonna continued. "You failed to invite me to the naming ceremony of your only child. I suppose you have a reason?"

"We didn't invite you because we thought you . . ." The king stopped. He had been about to say they thought she was dead, but he couldn't say that. "We . . . uh . . . thought you'd moved away. We're so glad you could come."

"Can I get you some refreshment?" the queen asked. "We have some deli—"

"I didn't move. Nobody thinks I moved." The fairy circled the cradle. "Some stupid people think I'm dead, but let me tell you, I'm very much alive."

"We have some delicious—"

"You can't buy me off with food. Maybe you figured the kid would get enough gifts from the seven of them." Belladonna waved her wand at the other fairies.

They drew back.

Belladonna went on. "You thought you'd economize—only buy seven gold plates, seven gold forks, seven gold . . ."

It's true, King Humphrey II thought unhappily. We do only have seven gold place settings, but because we thought she was dead. Not because we're stingy.

Queen Hermione II tried again. "There's plenty—"

"Maybe you thought I couldn't come up with a good gift. You thought I would run out of ideas, like Aurora here."

But I did think of a good gift, Aurora thought. How many people are ten times as smart as everybody else?

Belladonna roared, "You think I'm stupid like her? Is that what you think? Hump? Herm? Hmm?"

"Of course we don't think you're

stupid," King Humphrey II said.

"I'll show you I can think of a new and special gift." She leaned over the cradle. "Kitchy coo."

Oh no, Sonora thought, wincing at the furious face. Somebody stop her! Do something!

Everyone was silent, frozen.

I have to do it, Sonora thought. I have to talk her out of whatever she's going to do. "Excuse . . ." Her voice was too low. She'd never said anything before. She swallowed and tried again. "Excuse—"

Belladonna didn't hear. "Annadora gave the baby good health, which she will keep until my gift takes place. So my gift to the ootsy tootsy baby"—she waved her wand—"is that she will prick herself with a spindle and die!"

Two

When? Sonora wondered. When will I prick myself? When I'm eighty? Or in the next five minutes?

"I can't stay," Belladonna cackled. "I must fly." She vanished.

Queen Hermione II snatched Sonora up and held her tight.

Tears ran down King Humphrey II's face in rivers. What good was it being king if fairies could do this to you?

"It won't happen," the queen shouted. "I won't let it. You're not going to prick yourself with anything, sweetheart, baby dove."

Sonora wondered if her mother could prevent it. Or did it have to happen? If it had to happen, it had to happen. She'd just enjoy everything until it did. Sonora breathed deeply. Her mother smelled so good.

The fairy Adrianna coughed. "Nobody seems to remember that I haven't given Sonora my gift yet."

King Humphrey II threw himself down on his knees and clutched the fairy's skirts. Queen Hermione II put Sonora back in her cradle and threw herself down on her knees too.

"Please save our baby," the king pleaded.

"I can't reverse another fairy's gift," Adrianna said, freeing her skirts from the king's grasp. "That would cause a fairy war, and believe me, you don't want that. I thought of making Sonora artistic. What do you think?"

**"'I CAN'T REVERSE ANOTHER FAIRY'S GIFT,'
ADRIANNA SAID."**

"Can't you do anything to save her?" the queen sobbed.

"Tutors will teach her to draw and play the harp," the king said.

Adrianna went to the cradle. "Let me think." It was mean of Belladonna to kill the kid because of her parents' mistake. "I can change Belladonna's wish a little. She has to prick herself. I can't do anything about that. . . . I know." She waved the wand over the cradle. "Sonora will prick herself, but she will not die. My gift is that she will sleep for a hundred years instead of dying. Oh, this is brilliant!" The fairy beamed at the king and queen. "At the end of a hundred years a highly eligible prince will wake her by kissing her. How's that?"

Hmm, Sonora thought. A hundred years . . . her parents would be dead by the time she woke up! She started crying and howling and bawling. And wishing the fairy Allegra hadn't given her a loving heart.

King Humphrey II picked her up. "Funny baby." He bounced her up and down. "She doesn't cry when the fairy says she's going to die. But when Adrianna saves her . . ." He bowed to the fairy. "Then she cries."

"We can go to the banquet hall now," the queen said.

Sonora fought to catch her breath. She had to explain. "Wait," she said finally. "Wisten!" Talking was hard without teeth. She tried again. "Listen!" There. She'd done it.

The king's jaw dropped, and he almost dropped Sonora too.

"If I sleep for a hundred years, Mother and Father—" She started crying again. "Mother and Father will die before I wake up."

"She can talk!" the queen said.

"And what if I have a dog or—"

"You can talk!" King Humphrey II lifted Sonora way above his head. "The ibble bibble baby can talk!"

And Belladonna said I couldn't think of a good gift, the fairy Aurora thought, smirking. How many gifts make month-old babies talk?

"Don't let them die while I'm asleep," Sonora begged.

She's right, the queen thought. But we can't criticize Adrianna's gift. She could get mad and harm Sonora.

"Um . . ." Adrianna said. If she really wanted to help Sonora, she had to fix as much as she could. "Suppose I do it this way. Suppose, when Sonora falls asleep, everybody in the castle sleeps along with her."

"Excellent," the king said. "Except

sometimes we're in the courtyard."

"All right." She waved her wand. "Everybody from the moat on in will fall asleep and sleep for a hundred years." She chuckled. "Sweet dreams."

⚓ ⚓ ⚓

When the fairies left, King Humphrey II and Queen Hermione II had a long talk about the hundred-year sleep. They should have included Sonora, who would have had lots of good ideas. But Sonora was in the nursery, being rocked in her cradle by a Royal Nursemaid.

"Maybe it doesn't have to happen," the queen said, brushing away a tear. "We'll be very groggy when we wake up."

"We'll issue a proclamation," King Humphrey II said. "No spindles inside the castle."

"No needles," Queen Hermione II

17

added. "Nothing sharp. Maybe if *any-thing* pricks her she'll fall asleep."

"No knives. No swords. No tooth-picks. We'll build a shed and keep everything in there."

"Belladonna didn't say when Sonora would prick herself," the queen said. "She could be fifty when she does it."

"No prince will marry her if he knows she's going to nap for a hundred years," the king said. "He could be out hunt-ing, and when he comes home, nobody greets him. They're all fast asleep."

The queen agreed. "Besides, the servants would panic if they knew. The whole court would leave."

They decided to keep the hundred-year sleep a secret. They didn't think of telling Sonora to keep it a secret too, because they kept forgetting how smart she was. But they didn't need to tell her because she already knew. She'd figured it out ten seconds after Adrianna gave the gift. Now, while she lay in the darkened nursery, she was thinking it all over instead of sleeping. She'd save sleeping for her hundred-year snooze.

The fairy's gift would come true, Sonora decided. If her head could change shape and if she could become plump just because of a fairy, not to mention getting smart twice, then of course she'd prick herself and sleep for a hundred years.

Sonora also figured out that her parents would try to keep the gift from happening by hiding the spindles. But wherever they were hidden, she'd find them and take one. She wasn't going to prick herself by accident at the worst possible moment. No. She would do it on purpose when the time was exactly right.

Three

The Royal Nursemaids couldn't get used to Sonora. It was so strange to change the diaper of a baby who was reading a book, especially a baby who blushed and said, "I'm so sorry to bother you with my elimination."

In her bath, Sonora never played with her cute balsa mermaids and whales. Instead, she'd remind the Royal Nursemaids to wash behind her ears and between her toes. After the bath, she'd refuse to wear her adorable nightcap with the floppy donkey ears. She'd say it wasn't dignified.

The king and queen had trouble getting used to Sonora too. The king hated to watch her eat. It was unnatural to see a baby in a high chair manage a spoon and fork so perfectly. She never dribbled a drop on her yellow linen bib with the pink bunny rabbits scampering across it.

There were hundreds of things that the queen missed. Sonora never tried to fit her foot into her mouth. After her second word, "wisten," she never said another word of baby talk. She never drooled. She never gurgled. She refused to breastfeed. She admitted that it was good for her, but she said it was a barbaric, cannibalistic custom. Queen Hermione II wasn't certain what a cannibal was, but she was embarrassed to ask a little baby, even though she knew Sonora would be perfectly polite about it. Even though she knew Sonora would be delighted to be asked.

But then again, in some ways Sonora was exactly like other babies. She had to be burped like anybody else, although other babies didn't go on and on about how silly they felt waiting for the burp to come. And most babies didn't cry from shame when they spit up on someone.

Because of her loving heart, Sonora also cried whenever anybody stopped holding her. Queen Hermione II could explain that her lap was falling asleep from holding Sonora and the heavy volume on troll psychology Sonora was reading. It didn't matter. She cried anyway. It didn't matter either if King Humphrey II said he had to meet with his Royal Councillors. Sonora cried anyway. And when the king said she

was too young to help decide matters of
state, her loving heart and her brilliant
mind were in complete agreement—she
had a temper tantrum.

She learned to crawl at about the
same time as other babies, although she
was more of a perfectionist about it
than most. She set daily distance goals
for herself, and she only crawled in perfectly straight lines and perfectly round
circles. After a day of crawling practice, she once told her father that she
enjoyed watching "the miracle of child
development" happening to her.

Although her overall health was
excellent, sometimes she got sick just
like other children. Except other children didn't diagnose their own diseases
or tell the Chief Royal Physician what
the treatment should be. And other

children got well faster than Sonora, because other children listened when their parents told them to go to sleep. Sonora wouldn't listen and wouldn't sleep.

Most nights, sick or well, she'd crawl into the royal library. She could memorize five or six books in a typical night. Fairy tales were her favorites. The more she knew about fairies, she reasoned, the better off she'd be.

On nights when she didn't feel like reading, she'd lie in her crib and think up questions. Then she'd answer them. For example, why did bread rise? She knew about yeast, but yeast wasn't the whole answer—because why did yeast do what it did? The whole answer fit in with Sonora's Law of the Purposeful Behavior of Everything Everywhere.

Bread's purpose, she knew, was to feed people. It rose so it could feed as many people as possible. The reason jumped out at you when you thought about it correctly.

She decided that when her hand was big enough to hold a pen comfortably, she'd write a monograph on the subject.

Sonora didn't learn everything by reading and thinking. She also learned from the people around her. As soon as she could walk, she followed the Royal Dairymaids everywhere and asked them a million questions about milking. She watched the Chief Royal Blacksmith and asked him questions. She spent days in the kitchen with the Chief Royal Cook, until the Chief Royal Cook wanted to pound Sonora on her Royal Head with the Royal Frying Pan.

"SHE FOLLOWED THE ROYAL DAIRYMAIDS
EVERYWHERE AND ASKED THEM A MILLION
QUESTIONS."

Once she found out everything the Royal Dairymaids knew about milking or the Chief Royal Blacksmith knew about smithing or the Chief Royal Cook knew about cooking, Sonora would get to work. She'd read every book there was on the subject. Then she'd think, and soon she'd come up with a better or faster way to milk or smith or cook or do anything else.

She'd be very excited. If it was the middle of the night, she wouldn't be able to wait until morning to talk about her discovery, so she'd wake her parents up. This was always a disappointment. The king and queen were too sleepy to listen, and sometimes they were grumpy about being awakened. The king even raised his voice once, when she woke him to say she'd found a way to grow skinless potatoes, which would save hours of peeling.

Sonora would imagine the joy her improvements would bring the Chief Royal Farmer or the Chief Royal Cook or the Royal Dairymaids. But she'd be wrong—they were hardly ever pleased. They liked doing things the way they were used to, and they didn't like being told how to do their business by a Royal Pipsqueak no bigger than a mosquito bite.

Sonora couldn't understand it. She knew that the purpose of dairymaids was more than to milk cows. They were people, and people had lots of purposes. If her brain hadn't told her that, her loving heart would have. But part of their purpose was to get milk from cows, so she couldn't understand why they didn't want to do it in the best way possible.

In fact, nobody was nearly as interested in what Sonora knew as she wanted them to be. Even her mother wasn't. Often, while the queen wrote out menu plans, Sonora would talk about her latest research.

And for the thousandth time the queen would wish that Aurora had thought of a different gift. A simple one would have been fine, Queen Hermione II would think. An excellent sense of smell would have been good, or a pretty singing voice, which didn't run in the family. She and Humphrey II both sounded like frogs.

Then the queen would try not to yawn. What was the child telling her now? How to build the fastest sailboat in the world? But Biddle was landlocked, and even its lakes were small. A *slow* sailboat could cross the biggest one pretty quickly. Queen Hermione II's eyes would close then, and her handwriting on the menu would wobble.

And Sonora would feel terrible, even though she'd know her mother didn't mean to hurt her feelings.

It would be the same with the king. He'd be deciding which squires were ready to be knighted, for example. Meanwhile, she'd start telling him about a book she'd read, a book that had been in his library forever without his ever wanting to read a word of it.

He'd say, "Sonora, sweet, we're not as smart as you are. We can't think about knights and dwindling—um, dwindling what? What's dwindling, cutie pie?"

"Dwindling unicorn habitats."

"That's right, darling. Tell us about it later when we're not so busy."

Sonora would leave then, knowing that her father hoped she'd never mention a unicorn to him again—with or without a dwindling habitat.

A new proverb sprang up in Biddle. Whenever a Biddler asked a question that nobody could answer, someone would say, "Princess Sonora knows." Then somebody else would say, "But don't ask her."

And everybody would laugh.

Four

When Sonora was six, she read every book she could find on the art of picking locks. Then, on a dark night, she stole out of the castle and went to the shed that held the spindles and the other sharp things. The moment had come for her to get her very own spindle so she'd be able to prick herself when the time was right.

She set to work, ignoring the sign on the door that said, "Keep out! Do not enter! Private property! Danger! Get out of here!" It took her exactly twelve minutes to pick all ten locks and another fifteen minutes to very carefully remove the spindle from the first spinning wheel she came to. When that was done, she picked the spindle up with the tongs from the nursery fireplace and carried it very carefully back to the nursery, where she dropped it in the bottom of her toy chest. She left it there, under the toys her parents had gotten for the child they expected to have—the one who wasn't ten times as smart as anybody else.

⚓ ⚓ ⚓

Every year King Humphrey II and Queen Hermione II made a birthday party for Sonora, which never turned out well. The party for Sonora's tenth birthday began like all the rest. The lads and lasses had come only because they had to. They stood around in the tournament field, feeling silly in their party caps. Sonora tried to be a good hostess and make them feel comfortable, but every subject she brought up fell flat. Nobody wanted to discuss whether fairies and elves should obey Biddle's laws, or who was happier, all things being equal, the knight or his horse.

Nobody wanted to play any games either. They had played hide-and-seek last year, and Sonora had told them how to play it better. It had taken months to forget her advice and get their good old game back. The year before that she had ruined blindman's buff.

They all sighed, including Sonora. It would be hours before she could return to her latest project, finding out why things had colors.

Then she had an inspiration. She called for ink, quill pens, and parchment for everyone. When the supplies came, she began to interview each guest in turn. Sonora listened and took notes while everybody who wasn't being interviewed grumbled about how stupid and boring this was.

When the last guest had been interviewed, Sonora cleared her throat nervously. This was the first time she had spoken before an assembly. She said, "Silence." Gradually everybody got quiet. "From my notes, I see that none of you enjoys doing chores."

The lads and lasses groaned. Now the know-it-all was going to tell them how to be better children.

"Here are seven good ways to avoid doing them."

The lads and lasses began to write as fast as they could. During the rest of that wonderful party, which flew by much too quickly for everybody, Sonora told them how to stay out late to play, how to get even with their enemies and not get caught, how not to eat food they didn't like, and how not to go to bed at bedtime (Sonora's specialty).

When the party was over, Sonora told the guests to bring their homework next year and she'd do it for them. As they left, everyone told the king and queen that it had been the best party ever. King Humphrey II and Queen Hermione II were delighted. They told Sonora she'd be a popular queen someday.

But Sonora knew better. When the lads and lasses grew up to be Royal Bakers or Royal Chimney Sweeps, they'd dislike her advice as much as their parents did. And they'd laugh and say the proverb to each other. "Princess Sonora knows, but don't ask her."

The evening after the party, Sonora

36

moved out of the nursery to her own grown-up bedchamber, which had only one thing wrong with it—a bed. Sonora had argued that she didn't need a bed and didn't want a bed and disliked beds very much. It didn't matter, though. She was stuck with it.

Late that night, when everybody else was asleep, she used her new fireplace tongs to carry the spindle very carefully from the toy chest in the nursery to the floor of her new wardrobe. She shoved it all the way to the back and covered it with a pile of the nightdresses she refused to wear.

Then she tried to forget about the spindle and a hundred years of sleep.

⚓ ⚓ ⚓

The right time for Sonora to prick herself didn't come. And the more time passed, the less she wanted to do it. She was only a little frightened by the hundred years. What she was most afraid of was sleep.

She hadn't slept at all since the fairy Aurora made her so smart. She'd seen her mother sleep, usually when Sonora was trying to explain something. She'd seen her father fall asleep while listening to the Royal Minstrels after dinner. Sometimes Sonora yawned when they sang, but then she'd sit up extra straight and open her eyes extra wide. She'd stay awake because sleeping people were scary. They were right in the room with you, sort of. Their bodies were, but their minds weren't, which was creepy. Sonora loved her mind, and she wanted to know where it was at all times.

⚓ ⚓ ⚓

When Sonora was fourteen, King
Humphrey II and Queen Hermione II
decided on a husband for her, if she
didn't prick herself before the wedding.
They chose Prince Melvin XX, heir
apparent to the throne of the neighbor-
ing kingdom of Kulornia. He was the
ideal choice. Kulornia was even bigger
and richer than Biddle. Sonora would
be queen over a vast empire.

King Humphrey II sent a dispatch to
King Stanley CXLIV, the prince's father.
He also sent a portrait of Sonora. King
Stanley CXLIV sent back his answer.

King Humphrey II opened the dispatch
and read it. "King Stanley CXLIV has
agreed to the wedding," he told Sonora
and Queen Hermione II. "The prince is
coming for a visit." A piece of foolscap
fell to the marble floor of the throne

room. King Humphrey II picked it up. "Oh, look. Here's a letter from the prince." He started reading.

> My dear Princess,
> My father, King Stanley CXLIV, says I'm going to marry you. I believe him. He always tells the truth, so I believe him. If he were a liar, I wouldn't.

King Humphrey II nodded. "He sounds sensible."

He sounds like a fool, Sonora thought. The king went on reading.

> I believe in honesty. The fairies made me Honest when I was born. Besides, I do what my father tells me. If he says to marry someone,

I marry her. I'm Traditional. The fairies made me that too when I was born. Below is a list of all the other things they made me.

1. *Brave.*
2. *Handsome.*
3. *Strong.*
4. *A Man of Action. (I used to be a Baby of Action.)*
5. *A Good Dancer.*
6. *Tall.*

Plus Honest and Traditional, as shown above. I trust you will find me as described.

> *Honestly,*
> *Prince Melvin XX*

"Sweetheart!" Queen Hermione II said. "He's just right for you. He's handsome and you're beautiful. He's a good dancer and you're graceful." They would have so much to share. The queen felt weepy. Her baby was leaving her.

Sonora also felt weepy. They had nothing in common. Nothing important. The fairies hadn't made him smart. They hadn't given him a loving heart. Was it time to get out the spindle and prick herself?

Five

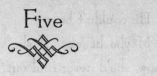

In her room, Sonora reached into her wardrobe. She touched the nightdresses that covered the spindle. Her heart raced. The moment had come.

But she didn't want to go to sleep.

Maybe the moment hadn't come. Maybe Prince Melvin XX wasn't so bad. His letter was so bad. But maybe he wasn't. Maybe he was just not a talented writer. He probably wasn't brilliant, but that might not matter. At least people wouldn't make up horrible proverbs about not asking him the things he knew. Besides, maybe he was really wonderful.

He couldn't be.

Maybe he was. If she went to sleep now, she'd never find out. He'd get old and die before she woke up. And she'd have missed the great romance of her life.

It wouldn't hurt to find out. He was coming soon. She could always prick herself after she met him.

♣ ♣ ♣

Prince Melvin XX came, following forty pages blowing trumpets. Sonora met him in the courtyard as he stepped down from his carriage. Probably he was handsome, but he was so tall she could hardly see his face, because it was too far away. He had dark hair and broad shoulders. She couldn't tell what color his eyes were. She'd have to wait to see them when he sat down.

She curtsied.

He bowed. He thought, I guess she's pretty. She's puny though. The fairies didn't make her Tall.

They had no chance to talk because they had to hurry to a banquet in the prince's honor. Sonora sat at one end of the banquet table with her mother. Prince Melvin XX sat with her father at the other end.

The prince ate, chewing very slowly. Sonora watched his mouth. He ate more slowly than anyone she had ever seen before. While he ate, he talked to the king. The prince spoke so slowly that King Humphrey II forgot the beginning of each sentence by the time Prince Melvin XX got to the end. Prince Melvin XX told the king about every second of his journey to Biddle. He explained how he had decided on each item he had brought from Kulornia. He said what he had been doing when his father had agreed to the marriage.

King Humphrey II wished there weren't so many courses. Another half hour of this and he'd faint.

The meal finally ended. King Humphrey II stood up quickly. "Sonora, sweet, show your guest the garden." Get him out of here!

Sonora curtsied and led the prince away. Queen Hermione II headed for her daughter's bedchamber to see what Sonora needed for her trousseau. The king decided to take a nap.

⚜ ⚜ ⚜

Prince Melvin XX held the door to the garden open for Sonora. "My father says you're smart," he said slowly. "And I believe him. He always tells the truth.

If he were a liar, I wouldn't believe him."

"That's reasonable." Sonora tried to smile, but she couldn't. I can't smile because I'm sad, she thought. If I were happy, I would be able to. Aaa! I'm thinking the way he talks. "Our roses are over here."

"I see them. The red ones are very red." He went on. "I'm glad you're smart. When I'm king, you can write my proclamations. I'll tell you what to say."

"If you tell me what to say, why—"

"Thinking gets in the way. People can be too smart. I'm a Man of Action. The fairies made me that way. I always know what to do. Father had to write a proclamation the other day . . ."

Sonora bent over to sniff a peony. Here was another person who would never want to listen to her.

❧ ❧ ❧

The king couldn't fall asleep. His head
hurt too much. Compared to the
prince, Sonora was a pleasure to listen
to. He rolled over onto his stomach.

❧ ❧ ❧

In Sonora's room, Queen Hermione II
began to take gowns out of the wardrobe
and spread them across Sonora's bed.
The child needed new ones for her
trousseau. Five or ten new gowns. The
prettiest gown Sonora had was blue,
embroidered with seed pearls. Where was
it? She turned back to the wardrobe.

❧ ❧ ❧

Sonora and Prince Melvin XX stood
next to the weeping cherry tree. He
was talking as usual. She had stopped

listening an hour ago. He was saying very slowly that he didn't see much use for flowers. Vegetables were different. He saw a use for them. He began to list all the vegetables he could think of.

Sonora wondered how bad sleep could be. A hundred years of sleep would be shorter than five minutes with the prince. As soon as she got away from him, she'd go to her room and prick herself.

No! If she did, he'd fall asleep too, and in a hundred years she'd still have to marry him. But then she wouldn't have a hundred years of sleep to look forward to. So she couldn't prick herself now. She'd have to wait and do it when he went back to Kulornia to get ready for the wedding.

"I especially like boiled corn in the . . ."

But meanwhile she didn't have to spend hours with him. She could think of an excuse to get away. She wasn't so smart for nothing.

"Do you like corn too?"

He'd stopped talking. He was looking at her, waiting. He must have asked her something.

"I'm sorry. What did you say?"

"I said do you like corn too?" Was she hard of hearing? That wouldn't be good. His own hearing was perfect.

"Not particularly." Maybe he wouldn't want to marry her if she didn't like corn.

"Oh." He shrugged. "I never met anybody who didn't like it before."

"Sir, I fear I must leave you for a while. The king likes me to use this hour for quiet meditation in my room. I will—"

"Corn might be my favorite—"

She fled.

♪ ♪ ♪

The queen lifted the last gown off its hook. Where was the blue one? Was that it on the floor of the wardrobe? She bent down to see. But it wasn't the gown. It was a pile of old nightdresses. How could the Royal Chambermaids have left them in such a heap? They could have been there for years. Queen Hermione II started pulling them out. She'd fold them up and shame the wenches with them.

Something underneath. What—

"Aaaaa! Aaaaa! Aaaaa! Help! Treason! Aaaaa! Aaaaa!" Have to get it out of here! "Aaaaa!" Protect Sonora! "Aaaaa!" She grabbed the spindle. "Aaaaa!" Had to run! She ran around the room, not knowing where to go. "Aaaaa!" The shed! She had to get it to the shed! "Aaaaa!" She ran out of the room.

Sonora heard her mother's screams and thought, Spiders! She started running.

Tarantulas! The screams sounded like they were coming from her own room. She thought, Black widows! I warned Father just last week. I have to reach Mother! I'm the only one who knows what to do if she's bitten.

The king sat up in bed. Was someone yelling?

The prince lifted his head. Someone was screaming. Was there a dragon? He looked up at the sky. He didn't see a dragon, so one couldn't be there.

"Aaaaa!" The queen raced down the north corridor, away from Sonora's room.

Sonora raced up the west corridor, toward her room. Let me reach her in time!

"Aaaaa!" The queen turned the corner.

"Coming! Don't wor—" Sonora turned the corner.

The spindle pierced Sonora's out-stretched hand.

"'AAAA!' THE QUEEN TURNED THE CORNER.
"'COMING! DON'T WOR—' SONORA TURNED
THE CORNER."

Six

In the meadow across the moat, Elbert watched his father's flock of sheep. It was a boring job. The only time it was interesting was when the castle drawbridge was lowered. Then Elbert could watch who was going in and coming out, and he could also see into the castle courtyard.

The drawbridge was lowered now. A team of oxen was crossing with a wagon-load of peaches. Juicy, ripe peaches. Elbert's mouth watered. Inside the court-yard, a butcher was cutting up a spring lamb. Elbert's stomach rumbled. He could almost taste it—roast lamb followed by peach pie.

On the drawbridge, the oxen stopped, and the driver slumped forward.

Huh? Elbert stared.

The driver almost fell off his bench. The heads of the oxen drooped. In the courtyard, the butcher stopped cutting. His head lolled to one side.

Arrows! Had to be arrows! Elbert spun around. No arrows were flying. He spun back. No arrows were sticking out of the wagon driver. None stuck out of the oxen.

He jumped up. Maybe he could help! Maybe he could get a few peaches and that lamb.

What was that? Something was growing along the outer rim of the moat. He started running. Whatever it was, it was growing fast—as high as his knee already. But he didn't have far to go. He ran faster. The hedge was as high as his waist. He'd jump over, grab the wagon driver, and drag him to safety.

He reached the moat. But the hedge was now up to his neck. He could still climb it, but he'd never get the driver out, and he'd get caught inside too. He stood before the hedge, panting. In his last glimpse of the drawbridge, Elbert saw one of the oxen switch its tail to brush away a fly. The ox was alive! It was—it was—asleep!

The hedge zoomed up, taller than Elbert. Taller than twice his height. Tall as the old maple in front of his cottage. Tall as the church steeple.

Elbert turned back to his sheep. Now

herding was going to be completely boring, without the drawbridge and courtyard to watch.

⚓ ⚓ ⚓

The queen's last wide-awake thought
was: The child will spend the next hundred years lying on a cold stone floor.

The king's last thoughts were: Our
headache's gone. We feel sleepy. We
could sleep for a hundred years.

The prince's last thought was: I could
take a nap. Sleep is good for you. My
father told me that . . .

Sonora's last thought was: Oh no,
I'll have to marry him. Aaaaa!

⚓ ⚓ ⚓

The fairy Adrianna appeared in the
courtyard. The hedge looked good. It

was high and dense and prickly, with thorns as long as her wand.

In the castle she stood over the sleeping forms of Sonora and Queen Hermione II. I can't leave them on the floor, she thought. She waved her wand, and the queen floated to the bed in the royal bedchamber, next to the king. Then she moved Sonora to her room and arranged her gracefully on the bed. She placed a wooden sign on Sonora's stomach. In flowing script it said, *"I am Princess Sonora. Kiss me, prince, and I shall be yours forever."*

Sonora wouldn't have liked that, not one little bit.

Prince Melvin XX was sneezing in his sleep, stretched out in a bed of clover. The fairy moved him to a wooden bench. Then she left without making anybody else more comfortable. They weren't royal, and they could make the best of wherever they happened to be.

In the next hour she appeared here and there throughout Biddle. She told everyone she saw that the royal family had gone on a journey. She said she had created the hedge to keep things safe while they were away.

Everyone believed her—everyone except Elbert the shepherd.

That night Elbert started building a very tall ladder, the tallest one in Biddle. A week later, when the ladder was finished, he dragged it to the hedge and climbed up.

The peaches were brown and rotten. The dead lamb was covered with flies. But everything else was the same. The oxen stood on the drawbridge, their heads drooping. The butcher leaned over his chopping block, the knife still in his hand. While Elbert watched, the butcher lazily reached up with his other hand to scratch his nose. They were all still asleep!

But why? Elbert wondered. Princess Sonora knows, he thought, but don't ask her. He laughed. Don't ask her because she's sleeping.

Seven

Sonora dreamed it was her wedding day. The great hall was filled with guests. Prince Melvin XX stood next to her. The Chief Royal Councillor was reciting the wedding ceremony. The prince hadn't moved once the whole time. He's like a block of wood, Sonora thought.

The ceremony was almost over. The Chief Royal Councillor said, "Prince Melvin XX, will you say a few words?"

The prince began to speak. Sonora saw a hinge at the corner of his mouth. She looked at his arm next to her. It was carved of wood! He was a big wooden puppet.

"Weddings are good. Everybody has fun at a wedding. There's always . . ."

Everyone clapped. Prince Melvin XX kept right on talking. Sonora screamed, "Aaaaaaaaaaaaaaaaaaaaaaaa . . ."

⚓ ⚓ ⚓

When Prince Melvin XX didn't return to Kulornia, King Stanley CXLIV sent a messenger to Biddle. The messenger came back and told the king about the journey the royal family was thought to have made. King Stanley CXLIV reasoned that the prince must have left with them. He wondered where they'd gone and hoped it was a good place for an Honest, Traditional, Brave, Handsome, Strong, and Tall Man of Action who was also a Good Dancer.

Five years passed. King Stanley CXLIV died, and Prince Melvin XX's younger brother, Prince Roger XCII, was crowned king of Kulornia. His first act as king was to annex the kingdom of Biddle, the kingdom without a king.

The saying "Princess Sonora knows, but don't ask her" spread from Biddle to Kulornia.

⚓ ⚓ ⚓

Queen Hermione II dreamed that Sonora was a little girl again. She was in the queen's lap, talking about the hissing turtle. Sonora said that the turtle hisses to fool people into thinking it's a whistling teakettle. Then why does the teakettle whistle? the queen asked. Because it doesn't know how to sing, Sonora explained. And Queen Hermione II thought, She's an extraordinary child.

⚓ ⚓ ⚓

Ten years passed. The shepherd Elbert's son Elmo was four years old. Elbert dragged his long ladder to the hedge again. He climbed the ladder with Elmo in his arms. "See," he whispered into his son's ear. "They're all asleep. Fast asleep."

⚓ ⚓ ⚓

King Humphrey II dreamed that he was writing a proclamation making the beaver the Royal Rodent of Biddle. He wrote each word as clearly as he could. But as soon as he finished a word and went on to the next, the letters in the last word changed. For instance, "beaver" changed to "molar," and "rodent" changed to "jerkin." It was very annoying.

"HE CLIMBED THE LADDER WITH ELMO IN
HIS ARMS."

Every few years, Elbert's sons and grandsons and great-grandsons climbed the ladder to look at the sleeping court of Biddle.

♧ ♧ ♧

Fifty years passed. Prince Melvin XX's grandnephew, Prince Simon LXIX, heir apparent to the throne of Greater Kulornia, had a son. Prince Simon LXIX's wife, Bernardine LXI, the princess apparent, invited the fairies to her son Jasper CCX's naming cere-mony. She invited all eight of them, including Belladonna, so no one would have hurt feelings.

There was trouble anyway. The fairies started arguing over who was the most powerful. Adrianna bellowed that she was the most powerful and she could prove it. So she turned the princess apparent into a shoehorn. Not to be outdone, Allegra changed the princess from a shoehorn into a baby troll. Then Antonetta turned her into a lady's wig. In the space of a half hour, poor Bernardine LXI became a piccolo, a crab apple tree, a quill pen, and a green peppercorn.

In the end they turned her back into a princess. But no one was certain if they had turned her into the same princess she was before. She was a little different from then on, maybe because one of the fairies had made an eensy teensy mistake, or maybe because the experience had been so terrifying.

Whatever the reason, when the princess apparent gave birth to a daughter two years later, no fairies were invited to the new baby's naming ceremony. Prince Simon LXIX worried about fairy revenge, but there was none. Each fairy blamed another fairy for the ban, so they didn't get mad at the prince, but they didn't give the child any gifts either.

And that was the end of the custom of having fairies at naming ceremonies.

♪ ♪ ♪

Prince Melvin XX dreamed about armor. He was polishing all the parts of his armor. While he polished, he named each piece. "One polished helmet. One polished visor. One polished haute-piece. One polished pauldron." And so on.

♪ ♪ ♪

Eighty-three years later, Prince Melvin XX's

great-grandnephew, King Jasper CCX, had a son, Prince Christopher I, or plain Prince Christopher.

Even though the fairies didn't give him any gifts, Christopher had a loving heart. He was smart, but not ten times as smart as everybody else. And he was handsome, pretty handsome anyway. But mostly he was curious. When he started talking, his first word was "why." And most of his sentences from then on started with "Why."

Why is your nose above your lips and not somewhere else?

Why are diapers white?

Why do you have nails on your fingers and toes? Why don't you have them anywhere else?

Why are peas round?

Why do birds have so many feathers?

He'd ask anybody anytime. The noble children of Kulornia liked Christopher, but they hated playing with him. If they were playing ice hockey, for example, he'd stop the game to ask why ice is harder to see through than water. If they were racing, he'd halt right before the finish line and ask why grass doesn't have leaves. Once, Christopher and his best friend, the young Duke Thomas, were watching a tournament. Just as the two champion knights galloped at each other, Christopher nudged his friend and pointed at a flock of geese flying above the stadium. "Look." Thomas did while Christopher whispered, "Why don't they flap their tail feathers too?" By the time Thomas looked down again, one knight was lying in the dirt and the other was trotting out of the arena.

Occasionally Thomas could answer one of Christopher's questions, but not often. Christopher's page could answer a few more questions, but then he'd be stumped. Christopher's tutors could answer even more, but then they'd be stumped. His parents could answer yet more, but they'd finally be stumped too.

When they were stumped, they all said the same thing. They all said, "Princess Sonora knows, but don't ask her." And when he asked who Princess Sonora was, they all told him it was just an expression. There was no such person.

It was the answer he hated most in the whole wide world.

Eight

As Prince Christopher grew older, he tried to answer his own questions. He read as much as he could in King Jasper CCX's library. He found some answers, but not enough, never enough.

Whenever his research got interesting, something always took him away from it. He'd have to practice his jousting. Or he'd have to try on a new suit of armor, or attend a banquet, where his father would forbid him to ask the guests even one single measly question.

A week after Christopher's seventeenth birthday, he was in the library, trying to find out if a dragon ever burns the roof of its mouth. A stack of books was piled next to him. He picked up the top one, *Where There's Dragon, There's Fire*. One of the chapters was about dragon skin. Did skin or something else cover the inside of a dragon's mouth? He opened to page 3,832.

A Royal Squire came into the library. "Majesty, the king wants you to come to the audience room."

Christopher slammed the book shut. It never failed.

Ten shepherds and one sheep faced the king in the audience room. As soon as Christopher took his place next to King Jasper CCX, the oldest shepherd began to speak.

"Highness, something terrible is happening to our sheep. See?" He pointed to the sheep. "She's going bald. They

73

all are. In the spring, there won't be much fleece for us to sell."

Christopher saw big bald spots on the sheep's back.

Another shepherd said, "In the winter, they'll catch cold. It's only October, and they're already starting to sneeze."

The sheep sneezed.

King Jasper CCX said, "God bless you." Then he called for his Chief Royal Veterinarian.

The Chief Royal Veterinarian spread a smelly ointment all over the sheep's bald spots. Then she gave the shepherds a vat of the ointment to spread on all the sheep.

A week later the shepherds and the sheep were back in the audience room. The bald spots were bigger. The sheep sneezed twice.

The Chief Royal Veterinarian told

"THE CHIEF ROYAL VETERINARIAN SPREAD A SMELLY
OINTMENT ALL OVER THE SHEEP'S BALD SPOTS."

the shepherds to keep putting the oint-ment on the sheep. She also gave them medicine for the sheep to drink.

Two weeks later the shepherds and the sheep were back. Now the sheep had no wool left, and she never stopped sneezing.

The Chief Royal Veterinarian shook her head. "I don't know the cure," she said. "Princess Sonora knows, but don't ask her."

King Jasper CCX asked Prince Christopher what he thought.

As usual, the prince had a question. "Could we send for all the shepherds in Greater Kulornia? Maybe one of them knows how to cure the balding disease."

It was done. Shepherds came from all over Kulornia and also from the land that used to be Biddle. Four hun-dred shepherds camped outside Kulornia castle. One of them was Elroy, Elbert's great-great-grandson.

King Jasper CCX talked to half of the shepherds, and Prince Christopher talked to the other half. The first one hundred and ninety-nine shepherds Christopher talked to said their sheep weren't getting bald and they didn't know how to cure the balding disease.

The last shepherd Christopher spoke to was Elroy.

"Are your sheep going bald?" the prince asked.

"No, your majesty."

"Do you know how to cure the balding disease?"

"I'm sorry, but I don't, your highness. Princess Sonora knows, but don't ask her . . ."

Christopher turned away.

". . . because she's asleep."

Christopher spun around. *"What?*

What do you mean, she's asleep?"

Elroy told Christopher everything. He told about the ladder and the hedge and the sleeping oxen and the sleeping wagon driver and the sleeping butcher. Halfway through the story, Christopher started jumping up and down, he was so excited. When Elroy was finished, Christopher ran to his father. King Jasper CCX was talking to his last shepherd.

"Sonora lives!" Christopher yelled. *"She sleeps! She lives! She can tell us about the sheep! She can answer all my questions!"* He shouted to a squire, *"Saddle my horse!"*

But Christopher was too excited to wait. He ran after the squire and saddled his own horse. Then he rode to his father.

"Sire! I'm off to old Biddle Castle." He galloped away, calling behind him, *"To wake the sleeping princess!"*

Nine

After two days of hard riding, Christopher and his horse saw the hedge. The horse reared up and wouldn't go a step closer. Christopher jumped off and walked the rest of the way.

The hedge looked wicked. It was taller than the castle back home, and it was full of thick, hairy vines and thorns like spikes and waxy red berries that practically screamed, *"Poison!"*

Christopher wondered what the name of the vine was and what the berries were like. He smiled. Sonora would tell him.

It was going to take days to get inside.

His sword wouldn't cut more than one vine before he'd have to sharpen it. Well, he might as well get started. He pulled the sword out of its sheath and walked toward the hedge, pointing the sword ahead of him.

It didn't touch so much as a leaf. A hole opened in the hedge and grew bigger and bigger until it was big enough for Christopher to step through.

Was it a trap? Was there really a princess named Sonora, or was a prince-eating ogress inside? Was Elroy the shepherd her messenger?

He had to go on. He had to find out—even if he died trying. He stepped through the hedge.

It snapped shut behind him. Oh no! It was as thick as before. He pointed his sword at it. Nothing happened. The hedge—or Sonora—wanted to keep him here.

He was at the edge of the moat. How was he supposed to get across? He could swim across if he was sure that the crocodiles were asleep, but he wasn't sure and he wasn't going to dive in to find out.

What? Lightning flashed out of the blue sky and struck a tree on the castle side of the moat. Whoa! The tree came down, making a rough bridge.

Christopher crossed slowly, stepping carefully between the branches. On the other side of the moat, he climbed a shoulder-high wall. Then he jumped down into a field of weeds so dense and tall that he didn't see Prince Melvin XX sleeping only a few feet away. The prince slept on the ground now. The bench he'd been lying on had rotted and fallen apart twenty years ago.

The weeds were brown and dying because it was November. Christopher wondered if this had once been the garden. He heard a rumbling. It stopped. There it was again. And again. Was it the breathing of the Sonora monster who lived in the castle?

He looked up. One of the castle's towers had crumbled, and an eagle perched atop another. Ivy climbed the walls. The pennants flying above the entrance archway were tattered rags.

Rumble. The earth trembled a little. *Rumble*.

Something rustled near Christopher's feet. Aaaa! A rat as big as a cat scampered across his boot. Christopher thought he should leave the garden. The bees were probably as big as pigeons.

Rumble.

The shepherd had said something about a wagon on the drawbridge and a butcher in the courtyard. He pushed through the weeds toward the entrance.

Rumble.

He reached the courtyard. There was the butcher! Possibly the Chief Royal Butcher, although you couldn't tell by the rags he was wearing. His shirt was so frayed and tattered that his belly showed through. He was slumped across his butcher block, next to a pile of bones. Fresh meat a hundred years ago, the prince thought.

And there was the carpenter, bent over a sawhorse, his saw at his feet. He was lucky he hadn't cut himself when he'd fallen asleep.

Rumble. Louder.

Or maybe the carpenter wasn't sleeping. Maybe they had all been turned to stone.

"Hey, wake up!" Christopher yelled. "Time to get up."

Nobody moved.

Rumble.

Christopher ran to the carpenter, who was closest. "Wake up!"

The man was filthy. His skin was coated with mud and dirt and dust and who-knew-what-else. Christopher wrapped a corner of his cloak around his hand. Then he pushed the carpenter's arm without letting his skin touch the carpenter's skin. The arm moved! It wasn't stone. He felt the carpenter's skin through the cloak. It was warm and soft—skin, not stone.

Christopher shook the arm. "Wake up! Listen! I command you, wake up!"

The carpenter slept on. He breathed in. His nostrils flared and his chest heaved. He breathed out, and the rumble started again.

It was the carpenter breathing! No,

it couldn't be. One person couldn't breathe that loudly. Christopher backed up so he could watch the butcher and the carpenter at once.

The butcher breathed in and the carpenter breathed in. The butcher breathed out and the carpenter breathed out—at exactly the same time.

There were more people in the courtyard. Two men, possibly nobles, had been standing and talking when they'd fallen asleep. A cobbler had been shaping leather on a last. A laundress had been washing a mountain of clothes. Rags now.

They all breathed in and out at the same time. After a hundred years, they must have gotten into the habit of breathing together. That was what made the rumble.

Christopher went to each of them. He yelled in their ears. He shook them.

He hollered, "Fire!" He yelled, "Food! Aren't you hungry?"

He yelled to the wagon driver and the oxen on the moat. But he was afraid to go to them. The drawbridge was rotting. If he stepped out on it, it might give way.

He tried to wake the dog, lying with his head on a bone. He tried to wake the cat. He told her about the huge rat that had run across his boot. The cat and the dog, Christopher decided, were sleeping because they were pets. The rats weren't pets, so they were awake.

Anyway, nothing worked. He couldn't wake anybody up.

What if Sonora wouldn't wake up either?

Ten

The castle doors were halfway off their hinges, so Christopher was able to open them only wide enough to slip through. Inside, he heard the flapping of wings. Bats. Birds too, from the droppings in the dust on the floor. He sneezed. He looked behind him, and there were his footsteps, sunk into a hundred years of dust. He took another step. His boots didn't make a sound because of the dust.

It was dim in here, in the great hall. The sunlight was weak through the grimy stained-glass windows. Even the broken windows didn't let in much light, because they were draped with cobwebs.

He crossed the hall. Where should he look first for Sonora, and how would he know her when he saw her?

People were everywhere, just as they would be on a busy day in Kulornia castle. "Wake up! Wake up!" he shouted. Nothing happened. He had stopped expecting anything, but he kept trying.

He shouted at everybody. But he shook only the women, and only women who looked like they might be a princess. He didn't bother with somebody who was making a bed or stirring an empty pot. He tried not to touch anybody with his hands. The people were all so filthy.

Nobody on the first floor would wake up, and it was probably useless to go upstairs and search the bedchambers.

They had fallen asleep in the middle of the day, so why would anyone be in bed? But he had come all this way, and he had waited all his life to get his questions answered. Besides, he couldn't leave even if he wanted to, because of the hedge. He returned to the great hall and climbed the staircase.

Most of the bedchambers were empty. But Christopher found King Humphrey II and Queen Hermione II on the bed in the royal bedchamber. It was sweet, Christopher thought. They were holding hands. The king snored so loudly that he probably made half the rumbling. What was left of the curtains fluttered whenever he breathed out.

Finally Christopher came to Sonora's bedchamber. Finally he came to Sonora.

Generations of spiders had spun webs

from post to post of her four-poster bed. Sonora slept under hundreds of layers of spiderwebs. The prince didn't know she was Sonora. All he knew was she was disgusting.

But she was probably noble, since she was on such a grand bed, or what used to be a grand bed. She might even be a princess. He had to do something. He coughed. Ahem.

Nothing happened.

He pulled out his sword and cut through the webs, which was a mistake. They all fell on top of her. Ugh. He brushed them away as well as he could with his cloak.

What was that on her stomach? Hmm, a wooden sign. He picked it up with his cloak and brushed it off. Dust and cobwebs and peeling paint came off. Drat! I should have been more careful, he thought.

He carried the sign to the window, where a broken pane let in a bit of sunlight. The paint had flaked off, but the wood was lighter where the paint had been. He could read it.

I am Princess Sonora. Kiss me, prince, and I shall be yours forever.

He didn't want her *forever*! And he certainly didn't want to *kiss* her.

Maybe he could live without getting his questions answered. He could train himself not to care so much. He'd hack his way through the hedge even if it took a month. They could find some other way to cure the sheep.

But what about all the people in the castle? And Princess Sonora, as sickening as she was? If he left, would they sleep till the end of time?

Let some other prince kiss her. Somebody who didn't mind getting ook and yuck and vech all over his face.

Who would that be?

Maybe he didn't have to kiss her. He touched her lips with the hilt of his sword. "Princess? Wake up. Your prince just kissed you."

Nothing happened.

He bent over her. He'd do it. But she wasn't going to be his forever.

What was that on her cheek and in the corner of her mouth? Spit? Bird droppings? Ugh!

He straightened up and turned to leave. He couldn't do it. He couldn't kiss her.

Eleven

"People float . . ."

Christopher whirled around. She was talking. She was awake!

Her eyes were closed. "People float because their essences . . ."

She was talking in her sleep. She had a sweet voice—a little hoarse, but sweet.

"People float because their essences are equal parts water and air. Stones sink . . ."

Even in her sleep she knew things! Sonora knows. And she was Sonora. And he was going to ask her everything.

He kissed her. He didn't think about

it. He just did it. It wasn't so bad.

It was suddenly quiet. Oh, Christopher thought, they're all awake.

"Sleep is pleasant." Sonora's voice was thoughtful. "Hmm. The purpose of eyelids is to cover your eyes. If you didn't sleep, your eyelids would have little reason to close, except when the sun was too bright. But then you could just put your hands over your eyes. That's right. If you didn't have sleep, you wouldn't need eyelids, so you have to have sleep. I made a mistake before."

Christopher was thrilled. She was answering questions he'd never even thought of!

She raised her head. "It's hard to open my eyes. I knew this would happen. My eyelids are covered with cobwebs and worse, aren't they?" She sat up slowly. "Do you have any clean water?"

"No. I'm sorry."

She opened her eyes and smiled at him. "You're dirty too."

Her eyes were big and gray, and her teeth were white against her dirty skin. Her teeth looked clean. The inside of her mouth was probably clean too, so she wasn't dirty all over.

He looks nice, Sonora thought. There was something smiley about him. He was sort of handsome, but mostly he looked nice.

He bowed. "I'm Prince Christopher."

Through the broken window, they heard people calling to each other.

She stood and swept a graceful curtsy. "I am Sonora."

"The sheep of some of our shepherds are getting bald. Do you know why?"

"Baldness in sheep is caused by scissor ants."

She did know! "Really! What cures it?"

"String is their favorite food, not fleece. To get the scissor ants off the sheep, the shepherds have to put big balls of string near where the sheep graze. The ants will leave the sheep and go to the string. Then the shepherds can take the string and the ants away and get rid of them."

This was wonderful! "Do you like to answer questions?"

She smiled again. "I love to answer questions." Then she looked sad. "Only nobody likes to listen. They don't even like to ask."

"I love to ask, and I love to listen."

They smiled at each other.

The sign says she's mine forever, Christopher thought. I like that.

Sonora read the sign in Christopher's hand. That fairy Adrianna! The nerve of

"THE ANTS WILL LEAVE THE SHEEP AND
GO TO THE STRING."

her! Sonora was about to say something nasty, but being so smart came to
her rescue. She'd never exactly *belong* to
anyone anyway, so it would be all right
if the sign gave Christopher a good idea.

It did. He knelt on the dusty, cob-
webby, bird-dropping-covered floor.
"Will you marry me?"

Sonora started to say yes. Her loving
heart loved this prince.

There were footsteps in the corridor.

She remembered. Prince Melvin XX!

The door opened. King Humphrey II
and Queen Hermione II rushed in.

"Are you all right, dear?" the queen
asked.

"You're dirty too," the king said.
"Who's this?"

"He's Prince Christopher," Sonora
said. "The sheep in his country are
going bald from scissor ants."

Christopher stood up and bowed. "I am Christopher, crown prince of Greater Kulornia, and I've just asked the princess to marry me."

"But Melvin XX is crown prince of Kulornia," Queen Hermione II said.

Prince Melvin XX? Christopher thought. But he disappeared ages ago. Oh! He fell asleep too.

"Our daughter is betrothed to him. He—" King Humphrey II stopped in confusion. What did this fellow say about Greater Kulornia? Where did the "greater" come from?

Sonora said to Christopher, "Since one of the purposes of sheep is to make wool, you might wonder if a bald sheep is still a sheep."

Christopher nodded eagerly. "Is it?"

She nodded. "It is, because its other purpose is to become mutton stew, and it can still do that."

"That hadn't occurred to me." He couldn't stop smiling at her.

There were slow, heavy steps in the corridor.

Here he comes! Sonora thought. What can I do?

Prince Melvin XX came in, ducking to get through the doorway. "I fell asleep," he said slowly. "I'm dirty. My hose are torn. So is my doublet. So is my crown. So are—" He saw Christopher. "Who is he?"

Christopher bowed. "I am Christopher, crown prince of Greater Kulornia." Did Sonora want to marry this guy?

Prince Melvin XX drew his sword—*fast!* "I'm crown prince of Kulornia." But he still spoke slowly.

Sonora thought, Put that sword away! Don't hurt Prince Christopher!

Christopher thought, He probably won't kill me if I don't draw my sword. "And I just asked Princess Sonora to marry me."

Prince Melvin XX thought, I can't kill him if he doesn't draw his sword. I'm not a Bully. I'm a Man of Action. I used to be a Baby of . . .

Nobody said anything. Prince Melvin XX lowered his sword.

Sonora felt a little better. At least it wasn't pointing straight at Prince Christopher anymore. She thought, I can think of a way out of this. I'm not ten times as smart as anybody else for nothing.

Prince Melvin XX said, "I'm betrothed to Princess Sonora—"

Sonora had it! "Sir Melvin XX—"

"I'm Prince Melvin XX. Not Sir."

Sonora shook her head. "We slept for

a hundred years, so you're not a prince anymore and I'm not a princess. You were betrothed to Princess Sonora, not to just plain Sonora. Right?"

"I don't know," said Prince or just plain Melvin XX.

She doesn't want to marry that great big tree trunk, Christopher thought. But does she want to marry me?

The king wondered if he was still a king, if Sonora wasn't a princess.

Sonora smiled at Melvin XX. "Your nature is to be strong and courageous."

Melvin XX nodded. "And Traditional and—"

She went on. "You will be a wonderful, traditional knight. You can have adventures and be brave and strong—"

"And Tall."

"And tall. I'm sure Prince Christopher would make you a knight."

Christopher didn't wait for Melvin XX to say yes or no. Usually Christopher did his dubbing with his sword. But he was afraid to draw it, because Melvin XX still had his out. So Christopher reached way way up. With his naked, dirty hand he touched Melvin XX on his forehead.

"I, Prince Christopher, dub you Sir Melvin XX, knight of Greater Kulornia."

"Now you won't need me to write your proclamations," Sonora said.

Sir Melvin XX said, "I will be a good knight. A Brave knight. A Strong—"

Christopher knelt. "I've always been curious, but I've never wanted to know anything as much as this. Will you marry me, just plain Sonora?"

"Yes, I will." She nodded and took his hand. "In case you were wondering, sheep grow wool because of winter. The purpose of winter is to make ice, so people can have cherry or lemon ices in the summer. The purpose of wool is to keep sheep and then people warm while the ice is being made."

"Really? That makes so much sense."

She looks so happy, Queen Hermione II thought.

"Are we still a king?" King Humphrey II asked.

"Of course," Christopher said, standing up. He'd work it out somehow.

Then it's all right, King Humphrey II thought. "In that case, we approve of the marriage. An excellent match."

Epilogue

As soon as King Humphrey II said he approved of the marriage, a gust of wind blew through the bedchamber, and the fairy Adrianna appeared. She beamed at everyone and crowed, "My gift was the best!" Then she married Sonora and Christopher on the spot.

After they both said "I do," and after they kissed, Christopher turned to Sonora. "Do you know if dragons burn the roofs of their mouths?"

"Yes, I know. No part of a dragon burns. You see, the essence of a dragon is fire . . ."

And they all lived happily ever after.

ALSO BY
Gail Carson Levine

Ella Enchanted
Dave at Night

THE PRINCESS TALES:
The Fairy's Mistake
The Princess Test